The Hatseller and the Monkeys

A WEST AFRICAN FOLKTALE RETOLD AND ILLUSTRATED BY

BABA WAGUÉ DIAKITÉ

SCHOLASTIC PRESS ▪ NEW YORK

Library of Congress Cataloging-in-Publication Data

Diakité, Baba Wagué.

The hatseller and the monkeys / retold and illustrated by Baba Wagué Diakité.

p.   cm.

Summary: An African version of the familiar story of a man who sets off to sell his hats, only to have them stolen by a treeful of mischievous monkeys.

ISBN 0-590-96069-5

[1. Folklore—Mali.] I. Title.

PZ8.1.D564Hat 1999   398.2'096623'02–dc21   [E] 98-16250   CIP   AC

10 9 8 7   03

Printed in Mexico   49

First edition, February 1999

The text type was set in Cafeteria.

The illustrations in this book were painted on ceramic tile.

Book design by Kristina Iulo Albertson

Special thanks to Anne Pellowski and Marilyn Iarusso for their help in leading us to early versions of this tale.

This book is dedicated to my two daughters, Penda June and Amina Marie, and to all the children of the world. They are our standing feet of tomorrow.

BaMusa the hatseller was a joyful man. He traveled from town to town selling hats, which he piled high on his head. "*Hee Manun nin koi kadi sa!*" he sang, which means, "What a wonderful business hat selling is!"

Ever since he was a little boy, BaMusa made and sold hats. His grandparents and his own parents were hatmakers, and they taught him to do this at a young age.

After each harvest, the whole family would venture out to the fields to collect rice stalks from which they made wide-brimmed *dibiri* hats to sell. During the rainy season, they embroidered close-fitting *fugulan* caps with intricate patterns of brightly colored threads.

Through his joyful spirit and hard work, BaMusa had become very well known in the neighboring towns. Wherever he arrived with his hats piled high on his head, children would follow him and sing along as he sang his favorite song:

"Hee Manun nin koi kadi sa!
Hee Manun nin koi kadi sa!
Hee Manun nin koi kadi sa!"

This is the story of how BaMusa learned an important secret for success.

One day, BaMusa heard that a great festival was to take place in a neighboring town. There, he could sell more hats than he'd ever sold before. He spent many days making hats for this event.

To get to the festival by evening, he began his journey in the early morning. But he was in such a hurry, he did not eat any breakfast. Halfway to town, BaMusa grew so tired and hungry, he had to stop and rest under a shady mango tree. He unloaded the hats from the top of his head and put them on the ground next to him. Then he covered his face with one as a blindshade to keep the sun from his eyes.

BaMusa soon fell asleep and began to snore loudly, *kuru tu-tu-tu*, *kuru tu-tu-tu*. Little did BaMusa know that the fruit from this tree attracted monkeys. BaMusa's snoring alerted them to his company.

As usual, monkeys are very curious and smart, and they crept down from the tree, *yolee, yolee, yolee* — quietly, quietly, quietly — and sneaked around BaMusa. Being attracted to the colorful hats, each monkey selected one.

Then they climbed back up the tree and imitated BaMusa, covering their faces and snoring, *kere té-té-té, kere té-té-té.*

Soon BaMusa awoke from his sleep, rested but hungry. Eager to continue his journey, he looked for his hats. *But where were they? Had they been stolen?* Frantically, BaMusa called for help. *"Hee Manun! Hee Manun!"* he cried out.

When the monkeys heard this, they answered him:

"Hoo, hoo-hoo!
Hoo, hoo-hoo!"

BaMusa looked up and realized what had happened. But he was so hungry, he could not think clearly what to do. He raised his arms in the air. "*Tchat, tchat, tchat!*" he yelled.

The monkeys stared down at him and replied, "*Hoop, hoop, hoop!*" shaking their arms wildly.

BaMusa threw a dead branch at them, hoping to scare them off.

But the monkeys merely threw leaves at him in return.

Then BaMusa picked up a stone and threw it up into the tree.
The monkeys picked mangoes and threw them down at
BaMusa.

By this time, BaMusa was faint with hunger, and so he collected the fruit and sat down to eat. He ate until his stomach was full. Now BaMusa could think clearly. Now he knew what he must do.

He removed the only hat he had left from his head and shook it up in the air at the monkeys, shouting "*Hee Manun, Hee Manun!*"

All the monkeys did the same, grabbing the hats off their heads, howling, "*Hoo, hoo-hoo! Hoo, hoo-hoo!*"

BaMusa dropped his hat *tot!* to the ground.

And all the monkeys dropped their hats *tot, tot, tot, tot, tot!*

Without losing a second, BaMusa collected all his hats, stacked them back on top of his head, and rushed to his destination. He arrived not a moment too soon.

So great was BaMusa's happiness from his recent luck that his spirit of goodwill helped sell all of his hats. And so it was that BaMusa learned from the monkeys: it is with a full stomach that one thinks best.

For an empty satchel cannot stand.

Author's Note

I first heard the story of "BaMusa and the Monkeys" in my home country of Mali, in Africa. The Fulani of Mali are by tradition cattle herders, and so, naturally, they are also milk sellers. A Fulani milk seller came to our family compound daily to sell us milk. One particular day, he arrived wearing two wide-brimmed, cone-shaped hats called *dibiri*. The children laughed, but the Fulani man said that, with two hats stacked, one gets twice as much protection from the sun and heat. My uncle, however, was reminded of the hatseller story, and, that evening, he told it to us.

There are many BaMusa stories in our culture, but this one is popular, as monkeys are always a favorite of both children and adults because of their humorous antics. In fact, Koroduga, who is the clown in mask dances, is represented by a monkey face. (Koroduga is depicted in the village festival scene of this book.)

Animals and man have been and still are instructors to each other in learning life's lessons. In this story, the monkeys cause the man much difficulty, but in the end they teach him that it is only after eating well that one can think clearly and enjoy success.

In many African tales, one must sometimes suffer before there is happiness. This helps prepare us for life. From childhood, we expect both happiness and some difficulty. This then teaches us patience and perseverance.

Stories are not only told as entertainment; but they give us knowledge on how to conduct ourselves and live among others and nature. I grew up listening to adults tell me proverbs and stories as advice to guide me through my own life. Teaching our children and setting a good example must truly be a duty for every adult, as children are our reflection.

RELATIVES OF *THE HATSELLER AND THE MONKEYS*

This popular piece of folklore has been told in various countries around the world, including Egypt, Sudan, Mali, India, and England. And the theme of a peddler having his wares ransacked by monkeys while taking a nap was a popular motif in European art during and after the Middle Ages.

Other variations of *The Hatseller and the Monkeys* can be found in the following books:

Bulatkin, I. F. *Eurasian Folk and Fairy Tales*. Illustrated by Howard Simon. New York: Criterion, 1965. (India)

Carpenter, Frances. *African Wonder Tales*. Illustrated by Joseph Escourido. Garden City, New York: Doubleday, 1963. (Egypt, Sudan)

Slobodkina, Esphyr. *Caps for Sale*. Illustrated by Esphyr Slobodkina. Reading, Massachusetts: Addison-Wesley Publishing Company, Inc., 1940, 1947, 1968. (Europe)

Willams-Ellis, Amabel. *Fairy Tales from the British Isles*. Illustrated by Pauline Diane Baynes. New York: Warne, 1960, 1964. (England)

NOTE

BaMusa's song, *Hee manun nin koi kadi sa*, is pronounced AYE MAH-noo NEEN KOING KAH-di SAH. *Hee manun* is both an expression of joy and a plea for help.